LITTLE
MO

Written by

Martin Waddell

Illustrated by

Jill Barton

WALKER BOOKS
LONDON

Little Mo looked at the ice
and she liked it.

BUMP!

Little Mo got up   and tried sliding again.

BUMP!

A Big One came to help her.

More Big Ones came out on the ice,

sliding and gliding around Little Mo.

They were her friends, all of them.

It was nice on the ice and she loved it.

The Big Ones whizzed and they whirled
and they twisted and twirled and
they raced and they jumped.

BUMP!   BUMP!

BUMP!   BUMP!

Little Mo started to cry and she turned away.
She didn't like the ice any more.

"It was all my idea,"
Little Mo said to herself.

The Big Ones got tired and went home.

They forgot Little Mo.

Little Mo looked at the ice
and she liked it again.

She slid and ...   and

and   she fell. BUMP!

She got up and then she
did it again without falling,   and again

and again

and again …

all by herself,
sliding about on the ice

and Little Mo loved it.